WICKED THROTTLE MC #0.5

By Esther E. Schmidt

Copyright © 2017 by Esther E. Schmidt All rights reserved.

No part of this book may be reproduced in any form,
without permission in writing from the author.

This book is a work of fiction. Incidents, names, places,
characters and other stuff mentioned in this book is the results
of the author's imagination. Corban is a work of fiction.
If there is any resemblance, it is entirely coincidental.

This content is for mature audiences only. Please do not read
if sexual situations, violence and explicit language offends you.

Cover design by:
Esther E. Schmidt

Editor:
Christi Durbin

Model:
Kevin James
instagram.com/Chicago_muscle

Photographer:
Golden Czermak / FuriousFotog
facebook.com/FuriousFotog
instagram.com/furiousfotog
onefuriousfotog.com

Laugh, cry, curse, words, no words,
poke, smack, love, lift, hug, we do it all.
We can be ourselves without restraints.
Lift each other up, grab by the nuts,
or kick each other's ass.

We're good in every way.
We're us in a connection where we're one.
Love you, babe.

I could say it a thousand times
and in a thousand different ways…
yet the meaning never changes.
Thanks so freaking much for yet again
supplying a sublime visual to wrap my work in.

**Dear readers, this model/photographer
is also an amazing author.**

Be sure to check out his books:
facebook.com/AuthorGoldenCzermak

Model & character…
it's hard to find an ideal match.
But in this case it was very easy.

Thanks so much for the flawless resemblance.
You've brought my character to life.

How the hell did I get myself into this? Oh, I know. The second I heard that heart-pulling whine, I just had to bend down and look into this fucking drain. When I locked my gaze with those bright eyes filled with fear, I didn't think twice and shoved my arm in there. Shall I mention the fact that my arm is massive? So now I'm stuck, just like that sweet puppy that my arm is keeping company.

Positive note is that the sweet little thing is kinda happy now. Cuddling, licking my skin...yeah, he's a good boy, or girl...damn, I don't fucking know.

I can't even tell what breed it is because my fucking arm is blocking everything.

Footsteps shuffle on the ground behind me. I can barely lift my head, because I'm lying flat on the ground and all, with my other arm tucked underneath my body. All I can manage is to turn it a little bit and get a glimpse of black biker boots. Wait, no…maybe they're SWAT or, hell I don't know.

Just fucking perfect, I can't do shit. Talk about a compromising position, with me lying helpless on the ground pinned to a damn drain.

"What on earth do you think you're doing?" If her voice didn't carry a punch, I might have written it off as timid.

Why? Why in the hell am I stuck and unable to look up to see if there's a nice set of tits attached to the body that produced that voice? Fucking excellent. Not only is my arm trapped, but my dick seems to be confined in my pants that appears to get a tighter fit with every passing second. Not to mention the fact that there's little space between me and the ground I'm draped over.

Ignoring the fucker that wants to get wet, and by this I'm not talking about the rain that's starting to fall, I try to think of something smart to say.

Except…there's that voice again. "Wait…you're stuck? Why would you put your arm all the way in there? And it's kinda big and all…not the brightest idea, but I think you've already noticed that little fact, right?"

Come on, I could really use a smart reply right about now, but the only head that seems to be working is in my pants. Isn't there a law against sexy voices when someone is in a rough spot or something?

I can hear her move and know she's looming over me. The sweet smell of jasmine and vanilla attacks my nose. This is pure torture considering I can almost feel the heat of her body so close to me…and that dog that's…

"Could you stop humping me?" I grumble in frustration.

There's a bite of pain due to a slap on my biceps.

"I. Am. Not. Humping you." She seethes and I

can feel her step away from me.

"No. Fuck, no. Not you, babe. The dog. The dog is humping my arm.

"There's a dog in there?" Her voice does have a bite to it, although this time it's filled with emotion.

I feel her crouching down next to me and then curly flames come into my line of vision. She's a fucking redhead? Great, just fucking great.

"Aw, you sweet little thing, I'll get you out. But first I need to get this huge chunk of biker out of our way, so hold on little one." She croons.

I'm still processing her words when she slides my other arm free that was tucked underneath my body.

"Grab hold of me." She instructs.

"Don't have to tell me fucking twice." I mumble.

Damn, I haven't even seen her and I'm already hooked to that enchanting voice.

My fingers find a loop on her jeans and do as I'm told. I feel her touch on my back as she presses me down against the ground some more. Probably to create more space and get a right angle to get my arm free. My cheek is now on the pavement and I see her pressing her boot against the curb with her knee slightly bent. Tight fingers wrap around my biceps.

"Hold on." She says only seconds before I see her leg go straight as a board and my arm is yanked loose. Hard.

Fuck, that hurt. Although I can hardly complain considering my arm is now free. There's that whine again. Shit, the dog is still in there.

"Move."

I'm pushed out of the way right after she throws that word out. Sitting up, I inspect my arm that has some lacerations. When I divert my gaze, all I see is a tight jean clad ass up in the air and a green shirt. Her magnificent red curls are about shoulder length and dancing around.

"I've got you, little one." She mumbles in an endearing voice while moving back.

There's a little bundle in her hands that might have been white at some point but it's dirty as fuck now. My eyes slide up and I am absolutely speechless. Some might not classify her as hot, but she most definitely is to me.

Those corkscrew flames surround her face. Eyebrows that are so perfectly arched that it appears she is questioning things. Her lips seem like they are locked in a forever pout. Full, pink, and I cannot wait to taste them. She's got a light spread of freckles on her cheeks and nose that look hot as fuck.

I'm still taking in every inch of her face even though it's blocked due to the puppy she's holding up to inspect.

"I think you're a Doberman pup, but you're all white… oh such pretty eyes…you're an albino, aren't you?" Her gaze locks with mine. "Don't you think?"

There's no air in my lungs. I might as well swallow my tongue because all of my bodily functions seems to seize with her standing right in front of me.

"Shit. You're bleeding too." She scrambles from the ground.

With the pup in one hand, she holds out the other

one for me to take. "Come on, let's get you cleaned up too."

My fingers wrap around hers and there's no denying the feeling of contentment that washes over me. Pushing myself off the ground, we keep our hands locked a moment longer than necessary. The pup starts to stir and she lets go to cradle the dog and walks off.

I see her tight ass stalk into the direction of the vegetable store. That's where I was going when I stepped off my bike and got sidetracked by the pup in the drain. My mom is in a retirement home and I visit as much as I can. I always come here first so I can buy her some strawberries or other fruit. I've never seen this chick here, though. There's always an old dude managing the store and talking my ear off.

Walking past a black GMC Sierra pickup truck, I follow the redhead into the store. She turns and shoves the pup into my hands.

"Can you hold him while I go grab the first-aid kit?" She doesn't wait for a reply but just jogs into the back and comes right out a few minutes later, kit in hand and a blanket in the other.

Putting the things on the counter, she walks toward the apples and grabs a box. She turns it upside down to empty it over another crate and walks back to take the blanket and puts it in the box. She grabs the pup, places a kiss on its head and gently sets him in the box that now clearly functions as a bed.

"Okay, let's do you first." Her words dropping like a bomb.

Yeah, let's do me. Right here? Shall I unzip my pants while you do the same? Damn, focus Corban, I don't even know her name.

"Before we get into you, or me, doing anything, let's make some formal introductions first." My hand comes up for her to take. "Corban Winspear."

Her delicate fingers wrap around me in a tight grip, she shakes twice and lets go. "Maud Gilford."

"As in 'Gilford's Fruit & Vegetables'?" The thought slips from my lips.

She gives a tight nod. "The very one. I'm the owner."

"The owner." I snort, because I always see the older dude here so I'm pretty sure her dad owns the store.

"Yes. Owner. As in working my ass off from the day I started, get up early, hard work and shit. That such a surprise to you, biker boy?" She bites out her words, clearly annoyed by the snort that snuck out, meaning I wasn't buying her being the owner.

And, really…biker boy? Okay…I am a biker, but I'm hardly a boy. I'm thirty-four years old… I'm a big dude at six foot four and my arms and chest are massive. Considering I'm wearing a tank and my leather cut, that obviously displays I belong to Wicked Throttle Motorcycle Club, along with the little patch she can't miss stating the fact that I'm the VP. As in Vice President of the MC. Clearly, I'm not a fucking boy.

"Do I look like a fucking biker boy to you?" I growl while I tower over her.

The pup starts to growl and jump, catching both of our attention.

She smiles down. "Oh, I'm gonna keep you. Such a good boy, already protecting me, huh?"

"Pretty sure he was protecting me, babe." I chuckle.

She crosses her arms in front of her chest, making my gaze drop to a perfect pair of pressed up tits. Nice.

"He's mine, I'm keeping him." Her face shows no room for disagreement.

Obviously, she doesn't know me. I never back down. Inching forward, invading her space some more, I lean down until our noses almost touch. "Then we'll divide ownership because the pup is mine too."

She rolls her eyes. "You make it sound like you're the Daddy and I'm the Mommy. Don't be ridiculous."

"That's right, we're doggie parents now. You're stuck with us guys. Ain't that right, Elmo?" Turning my head, I direct that last part to the pup.

He jumps up and barks. "See, he likes his name."

"Elmo? As in that red Muppet character?" She closes her eyes and shakes her head.

Spinning back, my lips almost touch hers. "Don't diss Elmo. He was all I got growing up."

"Fine." She seethes. "You picked the name so I get Elmo the first few days. I'll take him to the vet and you can come by here on Friday to have him for the weekend. Bring him back on Monday. There, parenting divorced-style."

Fuck that. "We will take him to the vet and I'll come over later to your house so he can settle in and get used to the both of us." I. Am. Brilliant. Thank you Elmo.

Her mouth drops open and she takes a step back. Elmo starts to whine, startling her out of her shocked state. We both squat down. The pup starts to lick her hand and switches to mine.

Maud looks up at me. "Fine." She grumbles.

I'm pretty sure my heart and dick twitched in sync by the sound of that single word.

"Are you gonna do me?" I can barely keep my face straight.

For a second she looks like she's gonna hit me before her gaze shifts to my arm.

"Shit. Yeah. Sorry." Maud swallows as she turns to grab the First-aid kit.

Her first reaction was the correct one, because she's for fucking sure going to do me.

CHAPTER TWO

"There, all taken care off." Maud states as she puts the antiseptic cream back into the First-aid kit and walks off to stash it away.

I check out my arm and yeah, she did do a nice job with cleaning it up and making sure it doesn't get infected. She walks back out with a bowl of water and a wet cloth. Bending over, she places the bowl on the ground. Maud gently lifts the pup out of the box and sets him down. Elmo starts to slurp up the liquid. Maud starts to rub the cloth over his fur to clean him up.

After a moment, Elmo's forgotten all about the water and is trying to grab the cloth. Maud beams the brightest of smiles before she hands me the cloth.

"Here, you entertain our dog. I need to get some work done." She stands up as Elmo tries to follow my hand while I spin the towel in circles.

I shamelessly watch her ass sway from left to right before I'm disturbed by needles piercing my skin. Fuck.

"Easy boy, no biting, ya hear?" I tell Elmo with a firm voice, making him release my hand from the tight grip of his teeth.

Scooping him up, I watch as Maud opens the back of her pickup truck. She leans in, grabs hold of a few crates and lifts them out of the truck. They look heavy as shit but she walks around with them like it's the most normal thing. She places them at the entrance on the left side against the wall. Walking back to the truck, she repeats the action on the right side of the wall.

Elmo and I watch as Maud unloads the truck and walks into the store with a few other heavy crates.

Dropping them on the floor with a loud smack, the pup yelps and catches Maud's attention. She strolls over.

"So sorry, sweetie. Mommy's not used to keeping it down and you're not used to my loud routine, are ya?" She croons.

Damn. She's so fucking close to me, her smell surrounds us as she leans in to kiss the fucking dog.

"Got one of those for Daddy?" One can try, right?

Her nose scrunches up in an adorable teasing way while her head gives a little shake. Then she surprises the fuck out of me when her hand comes up and cups my neck, pulling me down the same time as she rises on the tip of her toes to place a lightning flash kiss right on my fucking mouth. As if a feather brushes over my lips, leaving a tingly feeling all over.

"Fucking tease." I grumble.

Her soft snicker flows through the air as she steps away. Just before she walks out the door, she kicks against a few crates, making them align straight. And that would be the reason why she's wearing those kick ass boots instead of the fuck me heels I'm used to with the women who hang around at the clubhouse.

Not that she's like those chicks who will spread their legs for every single one of my brothers at any time. Pretty sure my days of random fucking are over too. This Mommy and Daddy talk is making me crave a step into the future. I want to settle with the things life gives you; a gorgeous woman to come home to and a family of my own.

Yeah, my brothers are my family. That's the reason I've been with Wicked Throttle MC for about fifteen years now. My dad was still a member when I became a prospect, he died before I was patched in. Bike accident, leaving my mom and my sister behind. There are only two of the older generations left in our club. And they are also the only two with Old Ladies.

So, if I was to claim this red-haired dog Mommy, she'd be the first of the new generation of Old Ladies. No fucking doubt about it, she could handle it, I'm sure. I make a mental note to invite her to the clubhouse on Friday. There's gonna be a party so that will most definitely either scare her away or settle her right in. That's going to be a very interesting sink or swim situation.

"What's that look on your face for?" Maud's voice brings me out of my thoughts.

Glancing her way, I see she's holding out a bag and is walking to the cash register.

Seeing no reason why I should lie, I might as well ask her right now. "You and me, party at the clubhouse Friday night, first date and all."

She turns the bag upside down on the counter and starts to count the money that she dumped out. Slightly annoyed by the fact that she's ignoring me, I step closer and stand across from her.

"See that, Elmo? Not even an hour together and Mommy is already ignoring Daddy. That's kinda rude, right?" Yes, I'm talking to my kid. Dog. Elmo, whatever.

Fuck, I swear every time she chuckles my dick jumps and there's this tight feeling in my chest that fills me with need.

"Daddy just needs to be patient. Besides, I thought our first date was tonight. Am I wrong?" She tilts her head, waiting for my answer.

"Nope." I lift the dog and I act like I'm having a secret guy moment with Elmo. "Better take note, dude. Mommies are always right. Even if they aren't…gotta keep the peace or we're going to get cut out of getting down and dirty time."

Lowering Elmo, who totally ignored my words and took that time to lick my face off, I meet Maud's gaze. Her eyes are clearly eating me up and that right there tells me the feelings that are coursing through my veins are most definitely mutual.

"You were right. Tonight is our first date. Your house, getting to know each other, without the fuss of the world around us." My voice comes out husky.

She takes a deep breath through her nose and holds it before she slowly releases. "Right. Well, I've made lasagna early this morning, so that's set. I'm waiting on…"

She doesn't get to finish her sentence because a

male's voice rings out through the store. "Morning, kiddo. Oh, I see we already have a customer."

Turning, I see it's the old dude who's always here when I come in. Honestly, I thought he was the owner.

"Hey, Corban. Damn, you're early today." The old guy states as he walks around the counter.

Maud is done counting money and leans over to grab Elmo from me.

"Eugene, meet Elmo...Elmo, this is Eugene." She drops the pup in the old dude's hands and Eugene needs to tilt his nose to the ceiling to prevent getting a tongue in his face.

"Aren't you a sweet dog, how did you get him?" Eugene pops out the question.

Maud takes our dog, fuck that sounds nice...our dog...and she starts to explain how we saved him. My mind is still skipping over in ecstasy about the fact that I'm having a first date tonight, and let me tell you... I've never been on a date in all my life, when I tune back in.

"…so that's why I'm not gonna work today and instead, I'm heading over to the vet to have him checked. I also have to pick up things I need for him, like food and a collar and so on." Maud's nose is scrunched up again and I'm sure she's mentally going over a list of things she needs to buy.

"Yeah, we're gonna drop my bike over at her place before we get in her truck and drive out to get the stuff for Elmo." There, I'm mingling into the conversation.

The old dude looks from me to Maud and back. "So, I see you've met Maud. I'm not so sure how I feel about you two getting together. You seem like a good kid and all, but…"

A good kid, what's with people today? Okay, I'm gonna check the first mirror I run into because clearly something ain't right with my appearances. That's twice I've been referred to as a fucking teenager. Besides that? I get the overprotective dad shit, but really, the few times a week I come here and talk to the old man doesn't give him the right to judge me.

Before he starts to spew out more garbage, I cut him off. "Look, I get you're looking out for your daughter and all…but she's a big girl and it's not like I'm gonna take advantage of her or something."

I might do some dirty shit and screw the ever-loving-fuck out of her, but I'll always put her safety and pleasure first.

"She isn't my blood, boy. But she sure feels like it." He eyes my cut for a moment before he continues. "I got out of the pen a few years ago, and no one would hire an old dude with a history. She did. Without a damned judgement or giving it another thought. I walked in and she hired me on the spot. Left me alone to manage the store with the cash in the register the same day. So, you get me when I say she's more than blood can ever be, right?"

"Fuck, yeah. That shit also means you know better than to judge on appearances, right?" I state.

We're eying one another as if we're both sizing each other up.

"Ooooookay, you guys. Glad we got rid of that

male bonding thing and all…but I never get a day off. So I'm gonna go and take care of Elmo if you got it all handled here, Eugene." Maud puts the pup into the box and picks it up. She heads toward the door. "Coming, Corban?"

Uh, huh…hard and fast the second I'm inside of you. Fuck, mind out of the gutter. "Yeah, be right there, babe."

I bring my attention back to Eugene. "I get it, man. She's special. I knew the second I heard her voice and didn't even see the rest. No need to throw out a warning." I grab a piece of paper and a pen that's lying on the counter and write down my full name, address, and phone number. "If there's anything you need or if something's up. Call me."

He gives me a look of approval before I'm out the door, heading for my bike, and for what feels like the next step in my life.

CHAPTER THREE

I put my foot on the ground after I've shoved out the kickstand and swing my other leg off the bike. Even though I mentioned earlier how we would bring my custom Harley Davidson V Rod to her house first, Maud decided we'd do it the other way around.

It's like she's doing it to stay in charge of things and for some reason, I'm okay with her taking lead on how she wants to handle stuff. Like now, she's out of the pickup and shoves Elmo and a set of keys into my hands.

"Can you open the door so I can get the stuff?" Yeah, she makes it sound like a question but there's no room for defying her.

For a dude who's only known the biker life, a small home with a white picket fence should be terrifying. Yet the feeling that overcomes me is clearly the complete opposite; it's like coming home. There's a small yard that seems to go all the way around the house and it's all grass. One glance and I can already picture Elmo running around, happily chasing a ball. I'm the one throwing that fucking ball, of course.

The second I turn the key and swing the door open, the intense smell of Maud surrounds me. Vanilla, jasmine…yeah, like I said…coming home.

Maud walks straight past me. "Can you grab the other shit I couldn't carry in one go? Oh, and you can put Elmo down, I've locked the gate so there's nowhere he can run off to."

I put the pup down before I make my way to the back of the pickup. Grabbing the last few things, I turn to see Elmo running toward me. Or at least he's giving it a good try. Ears flopping, it looks like he's jumping mountains to get to me.

We were glad the vet said he was okay, a little underweight but we got some special food to put some meat on his bones. The little pup now has a clean bill of health and a cool red collar with a nametag that says in bold letters Elmo. The fucking thing has both of our cell numbers on the back.

"Come on, Elmo…get your butt inside." It takes some effort to turn but then he's back to jumping mountains to get to me. His tongue is lolling out of his mouth, he's fucking adorable.

"So, everything went okay? Those kids try to steal anything today?…You shouldn't call them out on it, Eugene…I'm serious, they're just a little troubled. You know how Maci and I have a silent agreement." Her eyes meet mine and clearly she's talking to the old dude from the store. "Okay, well, next time I'll be there too. We'll handle it…Fine, I will. Bye Eugene."

She puts her cell away and shrugs her shoulders. "I had to make sure everything went okay."

"What's that about some kids you mentioned?" Probably nothing she couldn't handle, but I'm a protective dick so I need to know.

Shrugging her shoulders again, she clearly brushes me off. "Oh, nothing. Some neighborhood kids stirring trouble. Just a handful, but you know how boys are...they get together, have nothing to do around here so they gang up and throw some apples around or steal melons and run off. I cut them some slack last time but when Eugene is at the store they try to steal more on the grounds knowing that they can outrun him. He called them out on it but that just makes it worse. I know their sister, Maci. They're good people in a tight spot. That's all it is, really... like I said, kid stuff."

Elmo barks and jumps up, clearly wanting our attention. Reaching down, I scoop him up and step closer to Maud. Placing my palm on her right cheek to cup her face.

"When they get out of line with this shit, you call me, clear?" I give her a firm look to make sure she understands.

There's a slight nod and I can tell by the look in her eyes she's being honest. That right there is enough. Feeling Elmo stir, I lean in and place a kiss on his head, quickly dodging his tongue when he tries to slobber all over my face.

There's a slight mumble of words so it takes my brain a second to process. "Can Mommy have one of those too?"

Did she really? My gaze returns to hers and yeah, those pink cheeks tell me she most definitely just threw that out.

I let the hand that was still cupping her face slide to the back of her neck where I dig into those flaming curls and wrap them around my fist. Pulling her head back, I lower my lips to hers. Just before impact, I tighten my fingers and a little gasp leaves her mouth before I slam down.

My tongue slides in and I'm addicted the moment I taste her. I've kissed before but, shit... That doesn't compare to the intense pleasure that courses through my veins. Kissing is all about getting in the mood, the switch that flips to 'let's get it on'.

But this? Fuck. It's like getting plugged into an energy source that will light you up for years to come.

We both pull back at the same time when there's a third tongue slipping into the mix that's very large and very wet. Dammit, great fucking timing there, Elmo.

"Right. Let's feed the beast." She states.

Yeah, let me lock up the dog first so I can slide my zipper down and whip out said beast and shove it deep inside…dammit focus. The fact that she's sucking on her bottom lip while looking at me with heated eyes isn't helping one goddamned bit.

Her eyes glance down to where my dick is tenting my pants. "Food. I meant food. For Elmo. And us. I'm gonna…"

Yeah, clearly not the only one with their head in the gutter. She rushes to the kitchen while I put Elmo down. The little man rushes after her.

I let my eyes roam around the living room. Such a difference from what I'm used to. I mean my own room at the compound is more like a square box that only contains a bathroom, a bed, a dresser, a chair and a fucking TV.

But this? There's an L shaped couch that screams sit here, put your feet up and relax. A large ottoman in front of the couch to do just that. Lots of pillows for extra comfort. Most of the colors used around here are warm, earth tones varying from dark to light.

A small dining room table made from dark wood, sits with four chairs around it. There are a few paintings on the wall that don't make any sense to me. Other than a few interesting stripes here and there that might look like…yeah, no. I'm not gonna dig a hole for myself to contemplate the meaning with my wicked mind, because a shrink would have a field day with that one.

"Like what you see?" Maud's voice fills the air from behind me. Making me spin to look into those green eyes of hers that matches the shirt she's wearing.

"Now I do." I mumble while her cheeks turn pink.

"Lasagna will be done in about twenty minutes." She glances back toward the kitchen. "Do you want a beer, or something else?"

Fuck. You know what I want? I want to trade all my demons for one hell of an angel who sparks life with one hint of her smile. Yeah…sounds pretty fucking happily ever after to me. That's exactly what I want and need right now, and for eternity.

"I'd love one." I smile back and give her a wink that pinks up her face some more. Dammit that looks hot with those freckles, makes them stand out.

I follow her back into the kitchen where Elmo is eating in a corner, a bowl of water right next to him. It's like I walked straight into some kind of farm kitchen or something. I mean, I can't explain it other than that. The sink is shaped as two large marble shaped boxes next to each other that flows into the counter.

The tiny walls between the dark brown, wooden cabinets are covered with all different colors of tiles. Only the equipment is high-tech. Meaning the lasagna is cooking in one fine looking oven.

It's the kind of kitchen where you have your kids standing on a chair to bake cookies together while you fight who gets to lick the spoon. While I, of course, already ate half the cookie dough. Yeah… that kind of kitchen.

She walks to the fridge and grabs a beer, pops the cap and tips the bottle up to take a large swig. Damn. Ever since I've met her it's like every single detail about her flares shit up inside me. Although I want to jump her bones, I really think this has to go fucking slow. Just to build shit up right.

Her lips leave the bottle and instead of grabbing me a new one, she just holds out the one she was drinking from. That right there…perfect. I take the bottle and finish it in a few swallows before I place it on the counter. Crowding her against the fridge, I pick up where we left earlier; with me, dominating her mouth.

"Corban" Wicked Throttle MC #0.5

Chapter Four

My boots are right next to the couch and my feet are up on the ottoman, right next to hers. She's curled underneath my arm, flush against me while Elmo is sprawled over both of our laps. All of us have a full belly. Maud makes a mean lasagna and after doing the dishes, we walked around the block with Elmo.

After that, I suggested we'd watch a movie. Letting her pick one was a mistake because she grabbed The Fifth Element. Bruce Willis plays the role of Korben Dallas. That fucking smile on her face right before she pronounced that fucker's name the way

Leeloo says it. Then it sounds exactly the way you write mine. Hardening my dick in the process… spilling my name like that. She needs to be dragged over my knee so I could spank that tight ass.

Instead I bit my cheek to prevent from doing so, and not to burst out laughing. Eventually we settled on having a Die Hard marathon. Obviously, we both seem to like Bruce Willis. I could watch this movie a hundred times, probably have already. This is also the reason why I'm watching Maud instead of the TV.

My phone starts to buzz and I don't even have to look because I already know who it is. My Prez, Zerox. I sent him a text before we went to the vet letting him know that I would be out for the rest of the day and would swing by the compound tomorrow.

Pulling my cell out of my pocket, I answer on the third ring. "Prez."

"Are you that comfy inside a fresh cunt that yer spending the night? Ya might wanna give me her number, because that shit has never happened before. Makes me want to tap that one too, because you not returning home tells me this one might be laced with gold or something."

"Your dick ain't comin' near my Old Lady, Zerox." Those fucking words that I barked into the phone just now slipped right out without even thinking about it.

I don't give a shit if he's my Prez, or my friend since we were fucking teenagers, I ain't sharing Maud. Not now, not fucking ever.

"Wait, what? Fuck. Did you say those magical words, brother? That an official claim?" Zerox, my Prez's voice is filled with awe.

All of the guys in our MC have a different view on life and bump heads from time to time. In this? Old Ladies shit? Clearly when you feel it deep down in your gut, it's as real as it will ever be. A claim is for life and we always follow through.

Wicked Throttle is basically known for our claims and all of us are aware of that fact. Well… if you want to believe the few silver members that hang around the clubhouse. Some still have their

Old Lady and some have passed away, leaving them to live the rest of their lives alone. A Wicked Throttle heart connects only once, and beats solely for that woman.

Maybe that's the reason why no one of this generation has staked a claim yet. Kind of making a point that it's bullshit, this legend of love and claiming at first sight. Hell, some might even fear it. You know…having your dick locked, and the only key that fits is that one and only pussy. Well, now I know for sure. It's real. And no, I have no fucking fear, I'm embracing that shit.

"Yeah." I look down at green eyes that are clouded with questions. "Maud is my Old Lady. That's an official claim, brother."

Maud gasps and hits me on the chest, making Elmo rouse from his sleep and bark in the air as if he's defending us against an army knocking on our door.

"I am not old. I'm twenty-nine, dammit." She glares at me. "How old are you, anyway?"

She scoops Elmo up and pets him while he snuggles against her.

Ignoring Zerox, who's laughing his ass off on the other side of the phone, I answer Maud. "Thirty-four. And with Old Lady I'm not stating that you're old, I'm making a claim that you're mine, as in my woman."

Her pretty little mouth turns into a perfect zero, dragging my eyes over to shoot images in my head I really don't want while I'm still on the phone with my Prez.

"I'm gonna see you tomorrow, man. I'm bringing her to the party on Friday so you can meet her. Talk later." I don't give him time to reply because I hit the end call button as soon as the words leave my mouth.

"So, I'm yours, huh?" There's a satisfied grin on her face.

Leaning in, my hand covers hers while we stroke Elmo, together. "That's right. Mine. I'm staying the night, but there's one thing you need to know."

She tilts her head. "And that would be?"

"We ain't gonna fuck tonight."

The grin slides right off her face, making me chuckle because, damn…feels good to know she was kinda counting on it.

"I said not tonight, babe. Because up until now… when I met a chick my dick likes, the fucker would take over and I'd be fucking within the hour. The way you make me feel, my whole fucking body… the connection we have is different. So, no, I ain't gonna fuck you the same day we meet. But we will be, soon." Very damn soon seeing I'm bound to blow if I keep stalling.

"So, with what you just said…I should be thankful your cock didn't fill me up when we walked into my store, huh?"

Oh, for the love of God. "Keep talking that way and I'll strip you naked and tie you to the dining room table and wait until it's midnight to bury myself deep."

And now she's checking her watch. Fuck. Me.

"I'm gonna walk Elmo one more time, then we're retiring to the bedroom to get some shut eye." And hope to hell the night goes by within a blink of an eye.

Maud stands up and puts Elmo on the ground. She strolls into the kitchen, only to come back out, holding one single damn key.

"Guess you know how one of these works." She states as I wrap my hand around hers and give a little pull so she stumbles right into me.

"Yeah, babe. Thanks." I grumble right before I bite down on her bottom lip, making her hiss and giving me the opening I needed to slide my tongue right in.

She moans into my mouth and I'm only seconds away from pushing her against the wall and taking her right here. The only thing that stops us is Elmo's whine. We break the kiss and see him dart from left to right. Thanks for the cock-block, little man. It's the perfect reminder for the promise I made her not to fuck her tonight.

"Gotta go handle some little dude stuff. Get ready for bed." I throw out before I scoop up Elmo and head out of the house.

It's weird how you can bond within such a short time. Not only to Maud, but this little white fucker who's running circles like a race horse and the second a car backfires he runs straight toward me with his tail between his legs. Safety, comfort, a rock to climb on so you don't drown in a flood.

"Are you done for the night, Mo?" His paws dig in my shoulders as he washes my face.

Yeah, we're good. Strolling back to Maud's place, I mentally plot how I can move in with her. Within an acceptable timeframe without freaking her out or pushing her, that is. Using the key she gave me for the first time warms my chest.

That's a fucking nice first step right there. Happy to say she's the one who took it, because she could just as easily have given me her keyring to use instead. So now I have the way into her house on my keychain and I'm positive I've already gained a way into her heart, as she conveniently snatched up mine.

When I walk into the kitchen, I see Maud's already placed a warm water bottle in Elmo's kennel. He strolls inside and turns around a few times in a circle before he lays down and lets out a deep sigh. Closing the kennel, I hit the lights and walk off to find the bedroom.

A small ray of light coming from upstairs indicates that I will find what I need up there. When I reach the top of the stairs, it's a perfect guide to the bedroom. There's no sound, seems like this whole street is sound asleep. Standing in the doorway, I see Maud snuggled underneath the blanket with her eyes closed.

Yeah, I know it's kinda late and with her running her own store, I'm sure she wakes up early so she must be exhausted. Again, my heart tugs because she gave me, a rough biker dude she's known for less than a day, a key to her house. And she gave it with the knowledge that she could go to sleep, knowing deep down I wouldn't harm her.

I make fast work of stripping down naked and slip into the bathroom to wash up. There's a new toothbrush near the sink along with a towel. Damn fine and thoughtful woman I tell ya. Finishing up, I make my way toward the bed and take a moment to enjoy the vision of those red flaming corkscrews draped all over the pillow.

There's a chant going through my head that sets a rhythm. 'Mine'. Fucking lucky I got my arm stuck in that drain today to save that pup. Karma, right? One who does good gets good in return. Fuck, yeah.

The mattress dips as I slide underneath the covers. Maud turns in her sleep and finds my heat to snuggle close. One of her legs tangles with mine, it's then I realize she's naked. Her fucking tits are pressing against me and let me tell you something; it's a beautiful thing.

You know what's not beautiful? The taste of blood in my mouth, from biting my cheek to keep from blowing my load. Holy fucking shit. This is going to be one very long night.

CHAPTER FIVE

Maud's arm slides down and my whole body freezes. It's a contradiction. Please go down some more, wrap your hand around my dick and…dammit, stay above my waist, dammit. See? Like I said, contra-fucking-DICKtion.

Her lips touch my chest and she feathers kisses up while she moves her body to press flush against me. My head is still tilted back and my eyes are squeezed shut. Oh, yeah…I haven't slept one damn second because all I want to do is bury myself deep.

Why? Why did I have to throw out that one

insane statement about not fucking on the same day we meet? Oh, yeah…because all I want for the rest of my life is to do just that. She's the one, so I can damn well…okay, that's it. The feel of her soft pussy against my steel pipe, sorry…no other way to describe a hard on that's been like that for hours, is marking the limit.

"Condom or bare?" I hiss those three words through my teeth. I open my eyes and tilt my head to see her face. "I'm clean and always wrap up, but right now…I want you. Nothing unnatural in between us. Get me?"

Her eyes go down and she looks uncertain. What the hell? Rolling over and taking her with me, I loom over her and soften my face.

"You'd rather we use a condom? Fine, either way, babe. Don't ever feel like I'm pushing you or will do something you don't want. Okay? I'll even back off now if you're not ready." Swallowing deep, I feel the need to add, "Might have to use your shower to jerk off a time or two. But, yeah…I will always place you first."

Her fingers reach out and slide down my cheek. "I grew up in a small town…the few guys that were around were more like brothers to me, so I didn't really date. Then I moved here and started my shop and didn't have time. So, what I'm really saying is…" Her voice trails off and although I heard every word she said…it doesn't make a lick of sense because…

"Holy fuck. You tellin' me I'm gonna be your first and your fucking last?" I groan because, I'm not sure this is such a great thing.

Don't get me wrong, it is, but really? That's like getting a top of the line bike but there's a speed limit on every damn fucking road so you have to enjoy the ride and scenery.

I bury my head into the curve of her shoulder. "Best fucking gift ever. But shit. I wanted this to be hard and fast and then again, slow and long. Guess I will chew a fucking hole in my cheek before I can blow my load. Did I mention you're the best thing I ever got in my life? Dammit. I've done some dirty stuff and yet here you are…pure and all mine."

"Could we stop talking and start doing? I really don't know what to expect, so I'd like to get it over with since all I've ever heard is that it's gonna hurt like a bitch. So, to me your first option does sound like something we should do…you know, get it over with hard and fast so I can really enjoy round two?" She's got her bottom lip trapped between her teeth and looks so fucking gorgeous.

My dick is right at her entrance and I can feel how slick she is. No matter how I fucking tip toe around it, this is gonna hurt. My hands find hers as I place them next to her head and lace her fingers with mine. Keeping my eyes locked with hers, I lift up and rock inside with one hard thrust.

She gasps and closes her eyes while her body freezes up underneath me. I'm struggling just as much with the tightness my dick is strangled in. Holding still, my mouth covers hers as I pour every ounce of emotion into this kiss. The second our tongues meet, I can feel all the tension leave her while she solely focuses on the connection of our mouths.

Maud starts to grind against me and that right there is what I was waiting for. Slowly, I pull out of that tight heat and gently push back in. My teeth nip her tongue to keep her focus off track now. I want her to feel overwhelmed in every direction. The fingers of my right hand give a little squeeze before I let go of hers. Trailing in between us, I find her magnificent boob and cup it in my hand.

My tongue is dueling with hers when I take her nipple and give it a little pinch. The sounds she makes, the way she writhes beneath me. Fuck. I don't think I've ever felt this connected. It's like we're perfectly in tune with each other. When you randomly screw it's all about getting off. Although I always make sure the chick has an orgasm, this doesn't compare to anything I've done before.

She's giving this to me; her pleasure, her first time, her heart and fucking soul. And I'm damn sure going to take it. My insanity goes overboard at the same time she lifts her legs and wraps them around me. Her free hand is on my back, nails digging deep while the other is still laced with mine in a solid grip.

Pumping hard in and out, the sound of slapping, skin to skin that's slick with sweat. My groans and her chants of pleasure are a build up for what's to come. I find her bundle of nerves and slide tiny circles around it before I press down on her clit and she goes off.

Cum leaves my body and bursts into hers in hot strokes. I'm buried to the hilt while I bellow out her name. It's like flashing through clouds in heaven where there's nothing else except her and me. Utter bliss is flowing through my veins as the cum just keeps pumping.

Ultimately, I come out of my orgasm cloud and look down at Maud. Well sated. That's how she looks. I feel fucking drained so I drop and roll, placing her on top of me while my dick never leaves her pussy.

Right now, I can't think of anything else in the world. Her and me, in bed. Best sex I ever had and I for damn sure want another round. Except I know for fucking sure she's gonna be sore as fuck as it is.

That reminds me. "Gotta clean up, babe. Although we did talk condoms…got the disease part handled…we kinda skipped the kids part."

She pushes herself off me. "Shit." Panic laces that tiny word.

My hand softly strokes her back. "Calm down, love. We already have the dog and a white picket fence. We need time to build a family so we might as well start now considering you're not getting rid of me."

Maud drops herself against my chest. Snuggling to take a comfortable position. "You might have skipped the kids part, but I didn't. I was just remembering if I took my pill yesterday or not, biker boy. Don't worry. I'll check when I go make coffee. So yeah, I'm on the pill and normally don't forget…unless someone interrupts my day, I guess."

"Hmmm… be prepared to get interrupted every day from now on so you might as well stop taking the pill all together." I mumble out the words as I slowly start to slide in and out of her pussy that's slick with both of our cum.

Her eyes close while she clearly enjoys my cock. "Let's focus on us right now. Oh, and raising a dog first…because if you name a white Doberman after a furry red monster, I kinda don't wanna know what you'd name your kid."

I pinch her nipple, just for that statement. Elmo fucking rocks. "That would be CJ of course."

She rolls her eyes and places a hand on my chest. Trailing a nail to my nipple before she twists it. "Corban Junior. Uh huh. Like I said…Let's focus on us first because I'm not sure if the world is ready for a miniature Corban."

My fist finds her red curls and I tilt her head. Latching onto the skin on her neck to mark my prey. Making her gasp then groan long and low. Yeah, this is something I intend to do for the rest of my life.

Soft whining catches our attention.

"Oh, that poor thing. I need to take him for a walk." Maud throws out those words but doesn't stir an inch.

Makes me chuckle on the grounds that she wants to stay right here, with me. "I took him for a walk every two hours. Because it's almost been that long since he last peed…I say he just knows it's time for someone to come get him and give him some attention."

"Hmmm…well then, I think we got a few minutes…right?" Her hips start to move and my dick stands to attention who is still buried deep inside her heat.

"The way you're gripping my cock, love…I won't need another few minutes. One's enough." I groan. Because, fuck…she feels so fucking good.

Her legs slide up to straddle me. Maud places her hands on my chest and starts to ride my cock. All I see is a sea of red curls bouncing. Fuck. She's watching where we're connected. My dick sliding in and out of her pussy.

"Move that gorgeous head, babe. I need to see too." Yeah, my dick has been against it all night and inside of it and yet my eyes haven't seen a thing.

And there it is. A fine line of red curls. Best sight I've ever laid eyes on. Most cunts I've seen were bare or a get lost in the woods kinda thing. But this? Delicate, soft, precious…and all mine.

Burying my fingers into her hips to push her off and on my dick, my gaze stays on the place where our bodies connect. I feel her walls begin to clamp down the moment my balls draw up. I'm sure all neighbors in the surrounding area know her name but I'm throwing it out in case they didn't.

Fuck. I think I came even harder than the last time. We might need a few hours in between fucking so I can regain some fucking energy or something. This shit is draining the life out of me, but it's so fucking worth it.

Chapter Six

I just dropped Maud and Elmo off at the store. Not literally, I mean she drove her pickup truck and I followed her on my bike. But I certainly made a show of kissing her goodbye before I left. She needed to do her shop stuff and Eugene walked in just a few minutes before I left.

I know it's unnecessary to feel like I have to protect her because she's been handling herself and the store pretty damn good her whole life. But she's mine now and I always protect and look out for what's mine. I feel better knowing Eugene is there and she's not all alone.

Strolling into the compound, the smell of stale beer hits my nose. Normally I wouldn't even notice that shit but ever since I stepped foot in Maud's house? Yeah, big fucking difference.

"There he is. Where's our first of the new generation Old Ladies, Corban? We need to check if she's qualified and up for the job." Barlow pushes himself off the barstool and heads for me. Slapping me on the back. "You know I'm only messing with you, right? So fucking happy for ya, man. Gimme her name, you can spill that much, right?"

"Maud. Maud Gilford, and she's got this blazing corkscrew fire surrounding the most precious face." I feel my cheeks ache due to the smile that's plastered all over my face.

"Dude. All my ears reached was Maud and precious face. That shit in between? Were those even words? Sappy shit automatically turns to static in my brain." Barlow shakes his head. "Remind me not to get fucking pussy whipped, because you sure as fuck start to sound like a poet, man, with all the static my brain registered just now."

Quill stands up and tucks his dick inside his pants before zipping up. "You should open your ears, Barlow. Might learn a thing or two. Chicks dig that kinda shit. Makes 'em spread their legs faster. Ain't got nothin' to do with sappy shit or pussy whipped, but everything with makin' a cunt cream."

Barlow eyes the chick that's grabbing the bar to get off her knees. "Yeah, when we have ho's dropping on their knees without one word…I don't see the fucking need, man. My cock gets playtime without becoming a fucking poet. Cream or not, my spit works just fine if I want lube."

"It would spice things up, Barlow." The ho, Cindi, adds into the discussion.

"Wipe the cum off your face before you start to talk, Cindi. Might make your words a little more believable." Barlow shakes his head and turns to me. "See? I'm not cut out for that shit. My dick is made to rock and shock. There isn't one female up to tying that fucker down."

"Right there with you, Barlow. There ain't no cunt that makes my dick jump in her rhythm. Besides…if there would be…she'd have to be the queen around here. Hard fucking job with guys like Quill and Beecher and fuck…every last fucking biker here." Zerox's voice dominates the room.

"You needed me, Prez?" Beecher throws out from across the room.

We all look that way and, shit…I wish I fucking hadn't because the idiot is pumping his dick in and out of a ho's mouth. He's got her tied down, on her back, on a goddamned table. The ho's head is hanging over the edge so she can easily deep throat him. He's got her positioned like that because the idiot doesn't like to be touched by chicks. But clearly, he wants his dick taken care of. Yeah, he definitely knows how to make that shit work.

Quill tilts his head and his eyebrows raise in praise of the way Beecher has the woman strapped to the table. "Mind if I use that when you finish?"

"Oh for fuck's sake…see what I mean?" Zerox

rambles. "I need to get out of here, you ready, Corban?"

"Yeah, let's head out." Shaking my head, I stroll toward the door, hearing Zerox's footsteps behind me.

We're headed to the gallery to get things cleaned up. Zerox's got a new exhibition coming up in two months. We're just going to double check things because we own the gallery, and Zerox wants to clean out the room where he keeps some of his work. His inspiration, or hell…motivation, has been faltering lately. Either he's got too much shit on his mind or nothing at all.

Swinging my leg over my bike, I throw the question out because I'm kinda curious. "You working on some new shit yet?"

"Nah, man. No fucking inspiration. I need to get me some, fast. Two months and I have what, three pieces ready? Maybe I just have to lock myself up in the studio and not come out until I have at least twelve more." Zerox straps his helmet on and let his frustration out by burning rubber.

It's late afternoon before we're finally done with boxing up his old work and getting the gallery ready for the next exhibition. I check my watch and see it's about half an hour before Maud will be closing up her shop.

"You got somewhere to be?" Zerox slaps my back.

I grab the garbage bag off the floor and walk out back to throw it into the container. Turning my attention back to Zerox, I let him know. "Yeah, man. I'm heading over to my Old Lady's shop. Wanna come with?"

His face tells me he was kinda counting on it. "Hell yeah, lemme grab my shit and then we'll roll."

He disappears into the office and strolls back out with a black bag. Pretty sure he's got a sketchpad in there with his pencils and shit. We've been on the road together lots of fucking times and it's always the same black bag that comes out when we stop somewhere. Then he just sits down and within no time at all the guy finishes an amazing piece of art.

We both walk out to our bikes. It takes us barely fifteen minutes to get across town to where Maud's shop is located. Parking our bikes next to each other, I see three kids huddled near the store. That is until one of them grabs a watermelon and runs off.

"Fuck." I growl.

Because I can hardly grab my piece and shoot the fucker over some fucking fruit, let alone the fact that it's a kid...I do the next best thing. To my right is a crate of apples and with one throw I hit bullseye. The apple bounces off his head with a splat. Just as the watermelon hits the ground in pieces.

"Damn, brother. Great throw." Zerox compliments me.

"Why the hell did you do that?" Maud scolds, running toward us.

What the fuck? "Because the kid stole. Didn't you see?"

Her eyebrows go down in a frown. "Yeah, I saw. I also know it's one of the Meyer brothers."

"And?" I growl because seriously, what the fuck is with the she knows they stole and who they were.

She rolls her eyes at that single word. "And… their sister is working her ass off to get food on the table and raising her four brothers all alone in the process. So, I know they sometimes take a watermelon and Maci comes by on Saturday's to get her groceries and to ask if they stole that week. If so, she pays for that too." She jabs a finger in my chest. "Don't give me that look, biker boy. I run my shop my way, get it?"

My arm circles her waist as I pull her flush against me. "Oh, I get you alright." My husky voice strokes her ear.

She raises on her tip toes and presses her lips to mine. Stepping away all too quickly, dammit.

"Zerox. That's my Old Lady. Maud…this here is my Prez, also the one guy who's been my friend for as long as I can remember."

Her smile is bright when Zerox takes her hand. "Pleased to meet you, Zerox." Maud gasps. "Holy shit. You have that…what's it called? That thing with your eyes. Wow. One blue and one brown eye. Talk about an eye catcher."

"Maud" I growl, because come the fuck on, she's still staring at my Prez.

Zerox chuckles. "Heterochromia, that's what it's called, freckles."

Maud casts her eyes down and moves closer to me. "Right…well…I need to close up and now I have to drop by Maci's place because I want to drop off some fruit. She's having a hard time as it is, and even more since that Nero fucker is trying to pull the boys into their gang."

"What Nero fucker?" Zerox throws out just a breath before me.

"Nero Mills." Maud states before she turns and stalks back to the store entrance.

Fucking hell. "Eastside Posse." Me and Zerox state at the same time.

Maud steps on one side of an empty crate, making it flip up before she grabs it, preventing her from bending down. Fuck. That's sexy.

"Yeah, that Nero. He's been tryin' to get into Maci's pants too. Luckily she works out a lot and can throw a mean punch. She's been getting on his case the last few weeks because she will gladly kill him and do the time, just to prevent her brothers from either getting killed or going to prison for any felony Nero wants them to do." Maud takes a deep breath and lets it out through her nose.

Shaking her head, she starts lifting crates and brings them inside the store. Damn. It's on the tip of my tongue to tell her "Lemme do that." but I can't for the reason that she's been doing this for years and it's her fucking shop.

Zerox punches me in the arm. "Get the fucking fruit, we'll drop by this Maci woman. I need the intel because the fucking Eastside Posse is still fucking active."

He's right. We shut them down a few months ago. Or so we thought. We don't interfere with shit around town, but fuck…we won't stand around if gangs rise up and start dealing drugs and shit. Bet that's why Nero is aiming for Maci's brothers because they're young and can saunter through the streets unnoticed so they can distribute his dope or bring in new customers.

"On it." I throw over my shoulder at Zerox while I make my way inside the store, grabbing some crates along the way and setting them down inside. Not to show her a man should do that job, but I was going inside anyway so I might as well help out.

"Hey, babe. Can you get that fruit for Maci you mentioned? Zerox and I will swing by so you can close up and we'll be back before you're done." My voice makes her look up from stacking crates.

Elmo clearly hears my voice as he comes running around the counter and jumps straight at me.

A frown ignites on her face. "I don't think that's such a good idea."

"Come on, I hit a kid on the head with an apple. The least I can do is drop some shit off and apologize, right? I'll even pick up the tab on this one, I owe them and you."

She seems to ponder that shit over before she replies. "Okay, but only apologize if Maci can't hear you. I don't want to get those boys into trouble because Maci would have to yell at them all over again. She doesn't need that shit."

I stand up from kneeling to cuddle with my dog. "Okay, boss." I reply.

Her frown washes off as desire fills her gaze. "Hmmm, sure like the sound of that."

"Well hurry the fuck up so we can go home and you can boss me around." My dick jumps in agreement, clearly ready to be her slave for the rest of the day.

CHAPTER SEVEN

We're standing in front of the tiniest house on the fucking block. Although it seems well maintained, it's still a very fucking old house. Zerox steps up to the door and knocks. We hear footsteps approach and the door swings open.

A boy, about twelve years old, just stands there eyeing us. "Yeah?"

"Your sister here?" Zerox asks the kid, just as I hear shouting from behind us.

Turning, I see the three punks that were at the shop earlier. The one I beaned in the head with an apple taking lead.

"You think you can come kick our ass? Our sister will kick both of you off our lawn, so piss off." The ring-leader informs us.

Taking a step forward, I hold out the bag in my hand. "Shut it, idiot. I came to give you this. Now take it as my apology or I will take another apple and stuff it in that big fucking mouth of yours. Understood?"

The little punk nods and takes the bag from me. Clearly smarter than his mouth. Not turning down free food shows he's hungry. That, or he wants the discussion to end because I hear Zerox curse behind me. Turning, I see why.

"Did one of my brothers cause shit?" The tiny woman in the threshold questions.

She's got dirty blond hair that's wrapped up in a high ponytail. Strings have fallen loose and cradle her face. She's got a tight and toned body, and I notice, not because I'm checking her out…but mainly because she's only wearing some kind of workout bra and a very tight hot pants. Sweat is pouring down her face, tits and God knows where else because I'm turning my fucking eyes away.

My dick would have been hard the second my eyes would see her, except…he doesn't even twitch. But I can understand why Zerox was cursing since that fucker is sporting major wood. Seeing as his dick is hording all his blood to prevent his brain from working, I feel the need to take lead.

"Just dropping something off, ma'am. I'm Corban, Maud's old man." Reaching out my hand, she takes it in a firm grip, shakes it once and drops it.

"Maci Meyer. But you already knew that." She eyes my cut. "Old man, huh? Good for her."

"What's up with that Nero fucker and why the fuck would you come to the door like that? Asking for someone to tap those goods or some shit?" Zerox growls and he puts me on edge with his screwed-up words.

Seems like his dick has really drained his brain, keeping it from functioning.

When I try to shush them both, she steps up in Zerox's personal space and pops up on her toes because she's tiny as fuck.

"You go on and try to get a sample, pretty boy. See if you can get your dick within one inch of my naked skin." Her voice is so soft and even. There is no anger in it at all and yet, it is scary as hell.

Zerox leans down so his nose is touching hers. "Only my zipper is keeping my cock from touching your bare stomach, Captain Cookie."

The second his voice turns husky at the end with the endearment, she starts to throw punches that Zerox automatically dodges and blocks. For a few moments it seems like they're both just smacking each other's arms like a couple of kids, bitching. Then they're both grunting because the punches are getting harder so they need to work to avoid that shit.

Her brothers are throwing words out, one after the other, cheering on their sister.

"Kick his ass."

"In the balls."

"Come on, that's it."

"Hit 'em hard."

Right as I'm about to step in between, she stomps Zerox on the foot the same time she punches him right in the eye. Clearly thrown off balance, he steps away from her.

"There. Hope the brown one stays closed for a few days. What I wear in my own goddamned home while I work out, to blow off some steam, is my own fucking business, not yours. If you wanna have another discussion about it, I'd gladly shut that blue eye of yours too." She turns and starts to make her way back toward the house.

"Hang on." I try to steer clear of touching her.

She puts her hands on her hips and takes a defensive pose.

"Look, I came here to drop things off and Maud mentioned Nero. We ripped him and his posse apart a few months ago. We don't condone any fucking drug shit in our town." Making my point clear, I make eye contact with every single one of her brothers. "So, if you need any help or have any intel, just let us know."

Her hands fall from her waist, clearly relieved by my words. "That's good to know, but we're steering clear of that dirtbag. Right, guys?"

Her brothers mumble in agreement.

Eyeing us both, she throws out, "See? Okay, every one of you in the house. Now. And you two, thanks for letting me know and bringing the stuff from Maud."

Maci takes a step toward her house when Zerox holds up a piece of paper he seems to have ripped from his sketch pad.

"My number. Call if you need anything." Zerox sounds determent.

One glance at the paper, she tilts her head, looks at his cut and then catches his gaze. "Zerox. The president of Wicked Throttle MC himself, huh?"

"The very one." He growls.

"I always handle my own shit." She walks off without taking the piece of paper from his hand.

"Fuck. She's got an ass." Zerox growls.

"Heard that." she throws over her shoulder.

"It was meant as a fucking compliment so you sure as fuck needed to hear it, Captain Cookie." Zerox states while his eyes stay on her ass, totally missing the fact that she's flipping him off with both hands.

Her brothers follow her into the house and the one I hit with an apple flips me off as well before he closes the door.

"She's got an ass." I mimic Zerox's voice. "What the hell, dude?" I question the idiot that's still staring at the door.

I give him a shove to the shoulder and he starts his way toward our bikes.

"Fuck man, are you blind or something? The chicks I've met all have a flat ass syndrome or some shit, and this one is round and…you know, something to grab hold of with both hands." Zerox is holding up his hands as if he's sizing up the way he needs to place them on Maci's ass. "She's got like a toned body but her ass is really big, like a juicy pear figure."

"Stop talking, asshole. Juicy pear figure, you're either hungry or horny. Don't combine that shit. Let's stick to you're horny, since you haven't gotten your dick wet for months now." Just stating a fact. Besides that? I don't need to hear talk about some chick's ass. "I'm heading over to Maud."

He nods and waves his hand. "Yeah, go. I need to head over to the compound. Gonna lock myself up in my room, man. I need to sketch."

"Lemme guess…that chick's ass." My bike rumbles when I fire it up.

Zerox gives me a death glare while he flips me off. What the hell is that shit around here with people waving their middle finger up in the air?

Chapter Eight

Content. The last few days have been a nice flow of routine. Doing club business in the hours that Maud runs her shop while we spend all the other time together. Never thought it would turn out like this. White picket fence, my old lady, a dog...yet I've come to realize it's everything I will ever need in this life

I walk back inside the house with Elmo hot on my heels from his last walk for the night because we're heading over to the clubhouse for the party. Maud picks up Elmo, gives him a kiss and locks him up in his kennel.

All of this while I'm openly eating her up with my eyes. She's wearing these black tight jeans with her boots. Yeah, she doesn't need heels or some shit. I find her work boots sexy as hell because they suit her.

But the dark red, tiny lumberjack blouse she's wearing that's tied with a knot on her belly? Buttons barely closing so there's a hint of a black with dark red bra showing. Yeah…that right there had me running out of the house with Elmo because we need to head over to the compound before I say fuck it, and after that, fuck her.

And I can't due to the fact that it's an all-present, mandatory thing. Once a month we have these parties where every single member needs to be present. It's a family obligation, mandatory because a handful would always make excuses and therefor we'd never be entirely complete.

Zerox changed the rule. Be there or you're out if you miss the next time. No matter how long you've been a member. Respect the rules, respect the brotherhood. We unite. Ditch that and you're gonna end up the one getting ditched.

"Get in the car." It's a growl, because I can't keep my calm.

She raises her left eyebrow but takes her keys out of those tight as fuck pants and swings them around her index finger.

"Whatever you say, biker boy." Slides out in a fucking sing-song voice.

Taking the keys off that delicate finger, very gently I might add, I swat her tight ass and lock the door. The drive over to the compound is taking too damn long because Maud is bound to torture me at every turn. Her hand is on my thigh and way to close to my dick and yet, according to said dick…too far away.

The fire pits that are scattered all over the terrain come into sight and I park Maud's pickup next to a row of bikes. I give her the keys back while we make our way toward the building. She needs to head to work early tomorrow morning, therefor she's the one driving back. Fine with me because I could use a beer…or ten for that matter.

My nerves spike when the whores of the club come into view. I've told Maud how shit goes with this MC and she also knows for damn sure that I won't touch another chick ever again.

That doesn't help the slight feeling of unease running through me. Those ho's are competitive as fuck when it comes to needing a dick. Although some of my brothers are all about sharing pussy…those cunts like to grab any dick and hold on to it, any way they can, so it stays with them instead of hopping from one to the other and back.

Fingers slide into my ass pocket and without looking beside me, I know it's Maud's hand. I curl my arm around her and tuck her beneath it, squeezing her gently against my body.

Maud makes a strangled noise. "Your biceps is as big as my head, you might wanna loosen up instead of crushing me."

I falter and wrap my hand in her curly flaming

hair, pulling it back to slam my mouth over hers. Maud's leg hooks into mine while she rubs her pelvis against me. Making me wanna fuck her, right here, right now. The beauty is…I can do just that due to the fact that my brothers won't mind. The downside? I never can, or would, though. For the simple fact; I don't fucking share.

"Are you gonna devour her, or can you give me a hand?" Barlow's voice barks out behind me.

Dragging my lips away from Maud, I look back. "What do you need, man?"

He eyes my Old Lady. "The name's Barlow, can I borrow your old man for a second? I need a second opinion about the design I'm working on."

Maud raises an eyebrow, making me chuckle. I feel the need to explain, on the grounds that Barlow is behaving himself right now; being polite and all.

"Barlow here can carve a bear out of a log within ten minutes. He's one hell of an artist and at the moment he's working on a set of dragons for a Chinese restaurant." Maud's eyes widen a bit at my words.

"No shit? That's awesome. I'd like to see you work sometime." She praises.

Barlow's eyes go to the ground. "Yeah…see…I never…I work alone, okay. But I can show you some of the shit I've made if you want. Another time. I mean… it's because it's too busy and most of my great pieces are over at the gallery across town."

Maud gives him a warm smile in understanding. "I'd like that. Now, I'm gonna go look around." Her eyes lock on me. "You gonna come find me, when you're done helping Barlow?"

My fingers trail down her cheek. "Absolutely, babe. Be right there."

She walks off and I openly watch the ass, that belongs to me, sway out of my reach.

"Fine piece of ass you have there. Does she have a sister?" Barlow's voice pulls me back to him.

Shaking my head at his question. "Nope. It's just her."

Damn, those past few days, when we're together and not fucking? We talk. A lot. About everything really. She told me her life story, I told her mine.

Then we spent hours discussing shit we'd want in life. Shocking that we both have the same goals. Talk about two souls heading down the same path and colliding to aim toward the future together.

I give him my full attention. "What did you want my opinion about?"

Barlow's shoulders straighten and all of a sudden, he looks dead serious. "Zerox had me running a check on Nero. You know, throw a few lines out to see if the fucker's still active. One of my little birdies got back to me, he's a friend of a buddy of mine. Both are DEA and one went undercover to take him down. Gotta treat this carefully man. Zerox almost flipped when I gave him the file. Something about a chick and her brothers who needed to be kept out of that shit. That made me dig deeper and goddammit, Corban…I put a trail on that Nero dude…no worries, they kept their fucking distance…but it seems like he's obsessed with this Maci chick. He's trailing her without her knowing. I can't tell Zerox that little detail because he was already spitting fire when I gave him the headlines before I got to the latest intel.

This is bad man, we need to stay the fuck out of it. We don't need the DEA up our asses. And that most definitely will happen if we step in, to either stop Nero, or protect that chick. Best to steer clear and let them handle that shit."

Fuck. My hand finds the back of my neck and I let Barlow's words wash over me. This shit is bad. I've seen Zerox's art, that he's been knocking out like clockwork for the last few days. Ever since he saw that Maci chick, he's got his inspiration back. Not that he seems like a love-sick fool or something, not at all. More like the punch she gave him kick started his artistic side again.

He never even mentioned her but with what Barlow just said, it does fire up something if she's mentioned. Zerox has always been a dude who steps up for the good kind of people. Clearly Maci is struggling to do just that and it's a hard fucking thing in this world.

"Good call, Barlow. Seeing we're all here anyway…let's get everyone in church, we'll go over it.

I'm gonna go look for Zerox and talk shit through. After that, I'll let you know when to get everyone in so we can discuss what the fuck is going on in our town right under our fucking noses, yeah?"

He gives me a tight nod that I return and spin on my heel to make my way outside. After a few minutes, I find Maud and decide to keep my distance. Observing. Leaning back against the brick wall of the clubhouse, I enjoy the sight before me.

She's helping Zerox unload beer drums. There are six of my brothers standing around with their thumbs up their asses. Why? Because they are all gaping at my woman, who's lifting heavy shit, with her tits pressed up and her tight ass setting down those drums.

Quill steps forward, probably to help her out, meaning getting an eyeful of tits that belong to me. I've had enough.

"Maud, babe. You're way too good for that shit. You're helping out in more than just unloading the truck. My brothers are practically drooling and might run off to rub one out."

"Make that two." Quill states as he adjusts himself.

"Hmmm…I'm good at multitasking." Maud hums as she jumps straight at me.

I catch her with ease and lift her up, kneading that perfect ass in my hands. Her legs wrap around me and I can feel her locking her ankles by the way her grip tightens. She's looming over me when her lips meet mine.

Her tongue swirls around, making me groan when it meets mine. God, I love her taste. She puts up a good fight in a dual of dominance, but I'm the one that she submits to. As if she needs to make a point of who's in charge, she nips my bottom lip and pulls back.

"How long until we can run off and have crazy monkey sex?" She breathes.

Aw, fuck. "Wanna see my room?"

Maud tilts her head. "Does it have a lock?"

Hell. Yes. My talk with Zerox will have to wait

for about ten minutes. Two of those I will need to get to my room, four to eat her pussy and make her come, three to pump like hell to make the both of us explode and the other I'm gonna split in half…catch my breath and zip up.

"Zerox…" I yell over my shoulder. "You and me, talk in fifteen minutes."

Hear that? Decided I needed double time for pumping and two and a half minutes to catch my breath.

"Corban" Wicked Throttle MC #0.5

Chapter Nine

Kicking the door shut, I hold her up with one arm and flip the lock with the other.

"Dresser, chair, TV, bathroom, bed. Now you've seen my room." I throw her on the bed and her arms reach out to balance while bouncing on the mattress.

"Uhmm…nice place you have here, biker boy, real homey." Maud chuckles.

The sound of my belt unbuckling flows through the air. Kicking my boots off and a deep breath after that, my pants find the floor. I shrug off my cut and my camo tank follows suit. She's staring at me with desire blazing in her gorgeous eyes.

"This ain't my home, love. That's you. You're my home." I stalk the short distance to the bed and place one knee on it, making it dip so her body gently slides a few inches toward me.

"You give my soul the fearless comfort I've been seeking my whole life. You give me strength, hope, peace…everything you give me I intend to give back, tenfold.. I know it's quick, babe…but this is solid. Now, I've already married you biker style by claiming you as my Old Lady…but I need your signature to be my fucking wife. That's the only goddamn reason I'm asking." And that right there is frustrating. I would have had all the paperwork in order if I didn't need her consent. She's mine and mine alone for the rest of our lives.

Those fucking stories my dad and all those older generations of our club seemed like fairytales, made up bull about the 'once you see the other half of your soul, you claim that ride and make it yours'. But now I fucking know.

She's just staring at me, eyes wide.

"Say something, babe." My voice cracks with nerves.

Maud's throat bobs. "I think I love you." Her voice barely a whisper, those three words flowing out in a cough of dust but I fucking heard them.

"I'm gonna fuck the 'I think' right out of you. I'm not gonna make you come until I hear that line with only three words, am I fucking clear? 'Cause I damn well fucking love you." I growl while I rip those tight ass jeans off her legs.

"What the fuck is that?" I think my heart just skipped and my dick jumped.

She's wearing dark green boy shorts, not that fucking sexy but they look hot on her...but it's what's printed on there that has my body on edge.

"I think we were on the same mission tonight, so I'm kinda hoping that answers your question...no need to withhold my orgasm now...right?" There's a fucking smug smile on her face, I'm sure because I can hear it in her voice but I can't see it.

I'm still staring at her panty covered pussy. The words 'Corban's Place' written in big, bold letters. I don't fucking know how or where she had it made but we need more of those.

"We're gonna throw out the rest of your underwear and have a bunch of these in all kind of colors, ya hear?" I say in awe.

Maud chuckles. "I think we'll get a discount if you place an order above ten."

Fuck, yeah. My head slowly lowers between her legs. Those panties aren't coming off so I slide them aside and bury my nose into her cunt. Slowly sliding up and lapping my tongue along with it. I fucking love her taste and smell. My ride, my place, my fucking home.

She wiggles her pussy against my face when I cover her clit and suck, flipping that bundle of nerves with my tongue.

Letting go with a pop, I stare straight at her. "Loosen your blouse and pull up your bra, love. I need to see those tits."

Her hands make fast work so one of mine can slide up and knead one of those fine boobs in my hand, playing with the nipple between my fingers while I cover her slick pussy with my lips.

"Please, Corban…so close." She whimpers.

That sound makes me groan since I can fucking taste how close she is. "Gimme the words and I'll make you come, babe."

Her breathing picks up. "Yes, God, yes. I'll marry you, I'll love you, give me your fingers, your cock, your mouth…I need you, Corban. Give it to me."

So many fucking words between puffs of air going in and out of her body, just like my fingers are right now. She lights up the next second and comes all over my face. Her body shaking in my hands, screaming out my name and trying to grip my hair. Fucking useless due to the fact that's less than an inch on top.

Crawling up her body, I don't even have to grab my dick to place it at the right spot, because it's already there without guidance. Pushing forward in one hard thrust while her nails dig into my biceps.

"Hold on, love. This ain't gonna be sweet and loving. You've put me on edge and the need to blow is going to require a collision like no other." I growl, barely containing myself.

She doesn't give me one fucking word but just digs her nails in deeper. Fuck, yeah. My hand slides to her neck and I pin her with a tight grip. No fucking way I'm blocking her air supply, or hurting her, but enough for her to feel that I'm claiming what's mine. Body and fucking soul.

She's being pushed up the mattress with every rough thrust my cock gives her. Never straying my gaze from hers so she knows exactly how it works; it's not the long ride that binds us, it's the welcome home part. I might have thought I knew everything there is in life, but you don't fucking realize unless your life is complete.

I'm in a compromising position but it's so fucking good. The necessity to come is right on the surface. Yet, I am compelled to make it last all fucking night. My balls make a decision and her walls agree by clamping down. She screams my name and my voice tangles her name with mine.

Blissful pleasure courses through my veins and overwhelms me. Tilting her head with my thumb due to the grip I still have on her neck, I cover her mouth with mine. Slowly pumping in and out of her while I give her a sloppy wet kiss. Allowing our bodies to enjoy the aftermath.

Hard knocks on the door breaks our high. "Half a fucking hour ago you said fifteen fucking minutes, VP. I ran into Barlow just now. Get your dick out of your Old Lady. Church in five."

Footsteps die away and I have to chuckle because, yeah…I don't seem to fucking care about a time limit when I'm inside of my Old Lady. All the more reason to pull out because I need to handle business. My head tilts to the side while I'm still staring right at her.

"What?" Maud asks with an amused grin on her face.

Deciding to go with the truth, because that's what it's all about in the end. "I'm pondering how much intel you can and want to handle concerning club business."

The smile slides away and is replaced by a sincere look. "I will tell you all about my business, but I sure as hell would never let you tell me how to run it. I guess I would expect the same courtesy from you."

Fuck. Well I asked, didn't I? "Babe…you handle fruit and shit. Mine varies from Art to security, to kicking ass, and in some very incidental cases, but not entirely out ruled…blood and bodies. Get me?"

Not that we kill every turn we make, but it has happened in the history of our club where we run into rival gangs or like now, the shit with Nero… things could get sticky…meaning blood on fucking hands, sticky.

"The only employee I have is a guy who did hard time. I never asked what he did; everyone has their own reasons for the stuff they do. Darkness comes in many ways. We need the night time as well as the day time. Who am I to judge your balance between darkness and light? From everything you've shown me since you walked into my life, we share the same mindset." She never strays from my eyes. Every word with the same force as the next one.

I fucking knew she was perfect. I show the respect she just gave me with an intense kiss that is cut way too fucking short. I pull out of her sweet, hot and perfectly fucking tight pussy and leave the bed. Pulling on my pants, I start to lay shit out.

"Few months ago, we got up Nero's butt and ripped him a new one. We don't condone drug gangs in our territory. We thought we handled it but clearly he's getting back on his feet and thinks he's flying under our radar. Barlow found out that he's practically stalking Maci and we have it on good authority…" I look up from buckling my jeans, because she needs to be aware. "I know there's no need to say this…but babe…anything I tell you about club business is for your ears only, don't ever let it spill from your lips."

She rolls her fucking eyes. Yeah, that there is my answer…didn't need to lay it out.

The corner of my mouth twitches before I continue. "DEA is up his ass. So, we need to handle this shit delicately. They want to bring him down. We should stay out of it, but…"

"Shit." She jumps out of the bed and into her jeans. "I saw Michael and Morgan this afternoon, wearing new sneakers and jackets. Dammit, I'm sure that Nero fucker is spoiling them with stuff they can never get on their own so he can pull them into his gang. We need to do something."

"Yeah, about that…there's no we in this babe. It's me and the club." I drag her flush against my body.

I can see the struggle in her eyes. "I know but that kinda sucks, you know? Feeling useless in all of this. I can't just sit back. Maci will flip and won't stay out of it. I bet they change into their normal clothes at Nero's house, you know…to keep it hidden from her."

"You're probably right about that. I'll discuss it in church. Zerox seems to be on edge as soon as Maci's name drops. Did I tell you she gave him a black eye?" Thinking back, a chuckle leaves my mouth, because yeah...I didn't tell her that little part, Zerox threatened me if I mentioned it to anyone.

She gasps. "That's how he got the black eye?"

Now she laughs out loud and the sound is doing crazy things to my body.

"What lame excuse did he give you? The same as all the others, that he accidentally kneed himself in the eye when he was training?" Now I'm fucking laughing since the fucker can't even make up a good fucking excuse.

I mean who the fuck knees himself in the face while working out? Right. Idiot.

"Yeah and he made it sound like a joke so I believed him." Her laugh slides from her face and she turns serious.

Both of her hands slide to my head and she drags me down, taking my mouth. My arms cage her body and crush her against my mine. Fuck, I might never get enough.

Reluctantly, I come up for air and place my forehead against hers. "I love ya babe, and I really want to fuck you again but I'm needed in church about fifteen minutes ago."

"I love you too, Corban Winspear. Now, go handle some business while I plant my feet up somewhere."

"Lead the way." I grumble.

She takes a few steps toward the exit before I smack that tight ass of hers. "Be good." I command her.

She just fucking winks and strolls out the door.

Chapter Ten

"What fucking father would ever want every single one of his fucking kids' names start with an M? Michael, seventeen. Morgan, sixteen. Maximus, fourteen. Marcus, twelve. Maci, twenty-fucking-two." Zerox spits out that last piece of information like he's angry at himself.

I glance around the table where all of my brothers are gathered. No one seems to notice this little issue. Probably thinking the idiot is agitated over the fact that we have to deal again with this Nero fucker.

Barlow speaks up. "That's a good question but

we can't ask the dude because the father walked out of their life right after the last boy was born. They probably don't know but the fucker died. Shot by the cops during an armed robbery."

Damn. Yeah, with all the shit going on, it's probably a good thing to keep that little fact buried for now. No need to throw in more family drama. Zerox's eyes narrow and I'm pretty sure he's thinking the same thing as me.

He shakes his head as if to clear his thoughts. "Maci is putting up a good fight with trying to keep her brothers noses clean. Your intel, Barlow, states that she's the admin at an art and antique restoration company. She deals with all of the paperwork and customers so that the conservators can repair and or restore what comes in. It's a nine to five job so she can't keep an eye on them all of the time. She pays for everything and even that is a struggle. Now all of that is an invitation Nero gladly accepts." Zerox shrugs a hand through his hair.

I take this opportunity to speak up with the things

Maud just told me. "My Old Lady mentioned that Michael and Morgan were wearing new sneakers and jackets this afternoon. It's safe to say Nero is pulling ground to get those boys over to his side. Easy to bribe kids by giving them new shit they can't buy on their own. Letting them see how easy it is to earn stuff with just dropping off a package, no harm no foul, right?"

"That fucker is dead. I want him in the ground." Zerox throws out as he slams his fist on the table.

Every one of my brothers are looking at him in shock. Yeah, Zerox is always the calm one. That's why he works out. Beats the shit out of a bag every chance he gets to blow off steam. Hence the kneeing himself in the eye bull that he made stick to cover-up that black eye of his.

Me being the VP, and most importantly his friend, deep down I get the reason why he's on edge, I feel the need to step up. "What Prez is saying is that we need to handle this shit right now. DEA wants to take him down and we can't just sit back and think things over when these innocent boys with shit luck in life will be dragged into this while we can prevent it."

Quill ping pongs his gaze from Zerox to me. "He threw out he wanted to kill the fucker."

My annoyance spikes. "You can't condemn a person for voicing a thought that's in his head. Like I said, we need to deal with this fucker right now. As in kill his business without interfering with the DEA. We care about this town so we need to step up and protect the innocent youth this fucker is tainting. That's why Prez is acting so fierce, you know his fucking history."

Yeah, that was a nice cover up. Zerox was pulled into some shit when he was barely sixteen. We don't talk about that stuff but right now I can't voice my insinuations to my brothers. Clearly this Maci chick imprinted more than her fist in his eye.

"Yeah, what Corban is rambling about. These boys need someone other than their sister looking out for them. Our town, our fucking job. Clear?"

Zerox glances around the table to make sure everyone understands.

Quill stands up and walks to the fridge in the corner. A beer is placed in front of me and I chug the thing down in three swallows. This shit is getting to me and I'm ready to get crazy drunk and enjoy this evening and my woman.

It takes another hour to hash things out and when Zerox speaks up that the meeting is over, we're all relieved because no fucking decisions need to be made when you're intoxicated. Good thing we got the majority of it all hashed out before booze was starting to flow like a damn waterfall.

I make my way outside with Zerox right next to me. He eyes me with a look on his face that I can't quite interpret. "Thanks for having my back in there. I don't know about this Maci thing. Ever since I met her, I got my vibe back. Twenty fucking pieces ready for the next exhibition. She's my muse."

Snorting over that last piece he threw out. "Yeah, right. Keep calling her that, bro. Ya might start believing it yourself."

I can see the fight in his eyes to throw a fit over my words, except he swallows it down. Mainly because I shake my head and walk away. If he's not ready yet, who am I to force him to see things how they are?

That's when my gaze locks on her. Maud. My gorgeous Old Lady is sitting on a log while she's arm wrestling with one of the prospects.

I take a step forward to end this shit when Zerox fists my cut. "Don't you fucking dare. I need to see who wins."

Fuck. I'm kinda curious too, considering Nancy, the prospect she's about to arm-wrestle with, has the same build and height as Maud. That's why everybody calls the fucker Nancy. Delicate as a chick and yet he works out so underneath his clothes is a very lean body.

Another prospect comes up and hands me and Zerox a beer. Chugging the fucker down, I throw the empty bottle into a fire drum. One fucking second I take my eyes off my lady and she fucking wins.

Cheers call out all over while three whores turn their nose up in the air and stalk off. Yeah, that's the fucking difference between Old Ladies and whores. I'm sure if this club had other Old Ladies, they would have cheered for her and slapped her back. Just what my brothers are doing to her and Zerox to me.

"That's a fucking keeper alright." My prez adds in awe.

Stalking my way toward her, I manage to pull her out of the ring of brothers that surround her. "Amusing yourself there, babe?"

Maud throws her arms around my neck and keeps her lips a whisper away from mine. "Oh, yeah. Freaking funny to taunt those guys you call prospects."

"That so?" Rumbling those words out while my hands find her lush ass and swing her back and forth. I have to sidestep because, damn…I'm drunk.

"Wow. Seems like you're having a good time too." She throws out a laugh before she licks my lips. "I can't have a drink because I'm driving. Mind giving me a taste of what I'm missing?"

Letting one ass cheek go, I fist those flaming corkscrews and pull her head back. Sinking my teeth in her neck and sucking the skin so she carries my mark. She shivers in my arms and I have to pull away because the need builds to impale her on my cock.

"Go get me another beer, love. I'll wait right here so you can sit on my lap and kiss me when I've finished that bottle you're bringing me." I let her go and she stalks away.

Sitting my ass down, my eyes drift shut and I try like hell to keep them open. Damn. Those beers and fucking Maud in my room earlier drained the energy right out of me.

A hand slides down my chest and I can feel hair tickle my head. I take a breath and my eyes flash open.

Grabbing the hand, I throw it away from me. "The only woman allowed to touch me smells like vanilla and jasmine. You smell like trash. Fuck off. Respect a biker who has an Old Lady or get your ass thrown out of here."

I spit out my words because, fuck…talk about a bad fucking taste in my mouth. What if Maud saw her? Fear grips my heart when I find the eyes I was worried about locked on me. Zerox is standing right next to her with his arms crossed in front of his chest.

"See what I was talking about?" Zerox tells my Old Lady. "That's solid. One of the Wicked Throttle legendary truths. Once our soul finds its other half, there is no going back." His arms fall away and he shrugs a hand through his hair while they walk toward me. "All or fucking nothing at all." He grumbles, frustration rumbling through his voice.

Maud holds out the beer she got me. Grabbing it, I thrust the thing into Zerox's gut. "I'm done, we're going home." I try to raise myself out of the fucking chair.

Zerox grabs my elbow and drags my drunk ass up. "Yeah," He chuckles. "You're done, alright."

We both walk to Maud's pickup. Well…it might take me twice as long, on the grounds that I'm trying to walk a straight line here, but there are too many turns. Finally reaching the damn thing, I swing the door open while I hear Maud and Zerox talk.

"You need a hand with the big guy? To get him inside? I could tag along on my bike, if you need…"

"Nope." My gorgeous fucking woman states. "He'll either get into the house, sleep on the lawn or in the pickup. Either way, he'll be home." She chuckles while Zerox's laughter fills the air.

"I'm gonna eat your damn pussy, babe. Get in the fucking car 'cause I'm hungry." I grumble, because Zerox needs to mind his own fucking business.

"See? Or he'll fall asleep between my legs, whatever works."

Zerox's voice flows out one more time. "Yeah, one perfect sappy fucking match, the two of you."

I couldn't agree more.

Chapter Eleven

Something is tickling my nose but I really don't want to move because I love the softness I'm wrapped in, and the sweet smell of arousal that's surrounding me. Forcing my eyes open, thanks to the fact that I've got a killer headache, I find myself in the best fucking place of the house. Right between my woman's legs.

Oh, yeah. I wasn't kidding when I said I wanted to eat my Old Lady's pussy. Made fucking sure she came twice before my world went black. Lifting my head, I see she's still sleeping. Perfect. Breakfast.

Damn sure I'm gonna start right off where I finished last night.

I press down on her clit... kinda like keeping your finger on the doorbell. She stirs in her sleep and I'm getting to the part where the ringing of a bell makes you run to the door to swing the damn thing open... well, open up baby...your orgasm is waiting.

She starts to pant and I swipe my tongue lazily from ass to clit. Gasping she lights up like a fucking siren.

"Fuck yeah, good morning, babe. Hell of a wake-up call, don't you think?"

Groaning she guides my head back to her slick pussy. "Again, biker boy...I think I just fell asleep again." She groans.

Uh huh, addictive much? Ah, who cares? So am I. My teeth nip the nerve bomb that's peeking out from underneath her hood. Her pussy is all puffed up and slick, just the way I like it...ready for my cock.

I raise myself up to fuck her, except my head and body are clearly not up for it, so I fall down right beside her.

Her laughter flows through the room. "Seems I'm not the only one still sleeping, huh?"

"Fucking hangover." I mumble while I bury my arm underneath her and finding her hand on the other side so I lace my fingers with hers.

Sliding my other hand down her body to find that slick pussy that belongs to me. I raise myself on my elbow to steady my body and loom over her while I keep finger fucking her. My eyes are locked into hers to show Maud I'm the master that dominates her mind and her body.

The intensity of all of it surrounds us as she screams out her orgasm. I fucking love the fact that she comes alive underneath my fingers. It doesn't take much for her to light up like that and she takes all I give her and surrenders beautifully.

Damn. I really want to pound that pussy, except I have no fucking energy in my body. Falling to my back, I feel her letting go and loom over me. My eyes drift shut. I need a few minutes of sleep before I can get my body to work. That and a fucking aspirin or two.

My head raises because I need to fucking see that tight, heat that is now covering my dick. The sight before me makes me struggle for my next breath. Red flaming curls bouncing while green eyes are focused on me. Those lush lips tightening around my cock.

A primal growl builds deep in my throat, just like the orgasm that's bound to blow. "Fuck, babe. If you keep sucking like that I'm gonna coat your heavenly mouth with my cum."

She fucking hums. Waves of vibrations surround my thick mushroom head while she flicks her tongue underneath that sensitive spot. Holy fucking hell. I think this must be the mother of all blowjobs.

Both my hands wrap in those curly flames so I can guide her head up and down my length. I'm practically hyperventilating due to the intensity of the buildup that she's creating.

"I'm coming, love. Either swallow or pull back, because it'll be rushing out in thunderous blasts."

Suction increases as her lips tighten around me.

Fuck it. I pull her closer to my body and keep her head in place while I feel my dick pulse streams of cum down her throat.

Slowly releasing my grip, I watch how she lazily licks my spent dick clean. "That was so hot." She whispers to herself.

"Pretty sure that's my line, babe. And for the record, it fucking was." I pull her up so she's draped over my body.

I'm drifting off when I hear a phone ring. It's not my ringtone so I'm pretty sure it's Maud's. She crawls off me and grabs her cell from her jeans.

"Hey Eugene….what? Oh, shit…call Maci, I'll be right there…no, no cops, we'll handle it…yeah, I'm sure…okay…be there in ten."

She hangs up but stares at her phone. "That was Eugene."

Stalking toward her, I place my fingers beneath her chin and lift up her gaze. "What happened?"

"He was opening the shop when three guys came up with masks. They were shouting about getting revenge for one of their own getting hit on the head and then they shattered the window. Eugene managed to grab one, another ran off but the other one tried to get his buddy free. Eugene punched the guy and he went down." Maud curses and starts to pace the room. "Those two were two of Maci's brother's, Corban. The one that ran off was probably a guy from Nero's gang. Spurring them on. Dammit."

"Fuck. I started it with throwing that apple. I fucking bet they told Nero about it and he seemed to get them all ruffled up that revenge is the way to get shit done. Being your own boss and owning the town. Show them what you're made of shit." Dammit, I should have fucking known that was a possibility.

Ripping my phone from my jeans, I hit speed dial and Zerox answers on the second ring. "Shit hit the fan. Eugene, the old guy who works for Maud just caught two of Maci's brothers. They shattered the window of the store. I'm heading over there right fucking now."

"I'm already on the road, man. I'm three minutes out." Zerox throws out before the line disconnects.

Throwing the phone on the bed, I push my legs into my jeans and find the other shit I was wearing last night because I don't have the fucking time to shower and put on a fresh set. When I'm done, I tuck my cell into my front pocket, and see Maud is already dressed in her work clothes and pulled her hair in a messy bun. Dodging time to brush and clean up, just like I am.

"Let's go." I throw over my shoulder when I make my way out the door.

Maud follows me with Elmo on her arm while she throws me the keys with her free hand. Snatching them out of the air, I unlock and we jump in and head over to her store.

When we drive up, there are screams that could wake up the whole fucking neighborhood. Maci is leaning into Zerox's face and he's leaning right into hers. This is fucking bad.

"Hey." I bark to catch both of their attention.

"You two are on the same fucking side, what the hell you idiots?"

Both of them wrinkle their nose and are about to dive right back into snarling to one another.

Looking to my right, I lower my voice. "You take on Maci, I'll handle Zerox, yeah?"

My girl nods and walks up to Maci, glad to hear Elmo whine in the car, for the reason that we don't need him running around here right now.

The two brothers that Eugene caught are sitting on their asses on the sidewalk, both their heads are down in defeat. The other two are standing right beside them. Yeah, their sister probably gave them hell already.

"Calm down, Maci. We're all here to help. I'm not gonna press charges, I know Nero must have been the one who stirred them up. They're good boys." Maud's voice is calm and understanding.

Maci nods but the words don't seem to lessen her anger that is clearly directed to Zerox. "You're an angel, Maud. I won't forget this, you've been there more than once and I'm very thankful. But this baboon here…" She steps forward and jabs her finger in Zerox's chest. "Threatened to take my boys away from me."

What the fuck?

Zerox wraps his fingers around her wrist and gives a hard pull, making her stumble into his chest. "I fucking said I'll take 'em in as prospects and lighten your fucking load, Captain Cookie. Don't flip my fucking words around and turn them into something they're not. I'm trying to make shit easier on you, dammit."

"Your words are slick, pretty boy. My Pa taught me to never trust a fucking guy that isn't blood." She turns her gaze to her brothers. "Blood or not…seems like I can't fucking trust anyone of y'all."

Maci turns her attention back to Zerox. Her chest is heaving. "You know what? You can have 'em. For everything I've given them or how fucking hard I've tried to keep up. It's never going to be enough. I'm done. With all of you assholes."

She bounces her gaze between Zerox and her brothers. Thinking things through, trying to decide what road she should take, for the sake of all of them. Looking over her shoulder one last time, she bellows out to her brothers. "Don't bother coming home."

Her hands are clenching and unclenching beside her body. Zerox tries to reach out, clearly torn.

She steps back, away from his touch.

"Don't fucking touch me." We all watch as she stomps over to her car.

"She's gonna regret that, I'll make sure the feisty brat is mine." Zerox throws out and I'm sure he didn't mean to voice his thoughts like that.

"That an official claim, brother?" Oh yeah, I intend to exploit that little slipup.

He locks his gaze with mine and I can see the resistance and fury in his body, but the surrender is right there in his eyes. Uh huh, that's a claim alright, except he refuses to verbalize.

My arm reaches out for Maud's waist and pull her against my body. Squeezing my fingers in her thigh while I hug her close. Thankfully I've got what's mine.

As for Zerox?
Time will tell if he's either got the guts or the glory to take what is rightfully his...the legend of Wicked Throttle MC that's rooted deep into our DNA, to claim what is rightfully ours.

"Corban" Wicked Throttle MC #0.5

Esther E. Schmidt

Wicked Throttle MC
will continue in Zerox's story.

ZEROX
WICKED THROTTLE MC #1

"Corban" Wicked Throttle MC #0.5

My "B-team":
Neringa, Cathy, Tracy, Judy,
thanks for your opinions!

And to you, as my reader,
and let's not forget my editor and bestie
Christi Durbin… Thanks so much!
You guys rock!

Contact:
I love hearing from my readers.

Email:
authoresthereschmidt@gmail.com

Or contact my PA **Christi Durbin** for any questions you might have.
facebook.com/CMDurbin

ESTHER E. SCHMIDT

Visit Esther E. Schmidt online:

Website:
www.esthereschmidt.nl

Facebook - AuthorEstherESchmidt
Twitter - @esthereschmidt
Instagram - @esthereschmidt
Pinterest - @esthereschmidt

Signup for Esther's newsletter:
esthereschmidt.nl/newsletter

Join Esther's fan group on Facebook:
www.facebook.com/groups/estherselite

Join The Swamp Heads group on Facebook:
www.facebook.com/groups/TheSwampHeadsSeries

MORE BOOKS BY ESTHER E. SCHMIDT

MARLON

NEON MARKSMAN MC

PEACOCK
THE FAULTS OF OUR SINS

FREDERICK

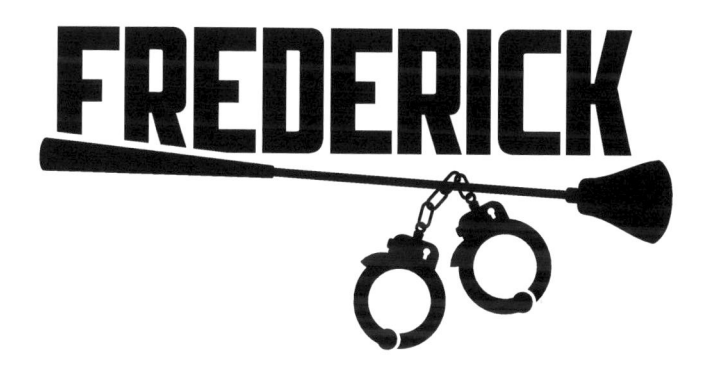

Made in the USA
Columbia, SC
28 August 2023